This book belongs to:

....

In loving memory of my father, Athol Raymond Owens.

And for my mum, Sue, my stepfather, Peter,
and my nieces, Olivia, Stella and Holly — Matt

For Evangeline Hudson, my artist grandmother, who
grew up at the beach shown in this book — Emma

This book is inspired by a true story, as featured on *The Dodo*.

First published in 2022 by Scholastic New Zealand Limited
Private Bag 94407, Botany, Auckland 2163, New Zealand

Scholastic Australia Pty Limited
PO Box 579, Gosford, NSW 2250, Australia

Text © Matt Owens, 2022
Illustrations © Emma Gustafson, 2022

The moral rights of the author and illustrator have been asserted.

ISBN 978-1-77543-764-2

A catalogue record for this book is available from the National Library of New Zealand.

12 11 10 9 8 7 6 5 4 3 2 1   2 3 4 5 6 7 8 9 / 2

The publisher would like to thank Fire and Emergency New Zealand and the Awhitu Voluntary Fire
Brigade for photo permission, p32.

Illustrations created in a mixture of hand-painted acrylics and digital painting on Adobe Photoshop
Publishing team: Lynette Evans, Penny Scown and Abby Haverkamp
Designer: Smartwork Creative, www.smartworkcreative.co.nz
Typeset in Minsins 17/24pt
Printed in China by RR Donnelley

Scholastic New Zealand's policy is to use papers that are renewable and made efficiently from
wood grown in responsibly managed forests, so as to minimise its environmental footprint.

The story of SWOOP

Inspired by a TRUE animal rescue

Written by
Matt Owens

Illustrated by
Emma Gustafson

SCHOLASTIC
AUCKLAND SYDNEY NEW YORK LONDON TORONTO
MEXICO CITY NEW DELHI HONG KONG

Enjoy the Journey

— Matt Owens

As firefighter Matt drove down the country road, something in his rear-view mirror caught his eye. He pulled over and got out of the firetruck.

There on the side of the road huddled a baby bird. It was a little magpie – cold, hungry and all alone. Firefighter Matt could see it was injured, and too young to fly.

"Don't worry, little one, I'll take care of you," Matt said, as he scooped the chick up in his gloved hands.

The baby bird survived the night. And the next day, she gobbled up the breakfast of mushy cat biscuits that Matt gave her. She seemed to be feeling quite safe in her new home.

"You need a name," Matt said. "I'm going to call you **Swoop**."

"**Squawk-squawk**," sang Swoop. It sounded as if she was happy with her new name.

But firefighter Matt also had a cat, whose name was Mogli. Matt was a little worried about how his cat would react to Swoop.

As for Swoop, well, she had never seen a cat before so she was very curious – and perhaps a little nervous.

Matt introduced them, speaking to Mogli in a firm voice. "Mogli, this is Swoop. Swoop, this is Mogli. Swoop's your little sister now, Mogli. She's **family**."

Mogli looked at Swoop with curious eyes. He appeared happy to have a little sister. And Swoop looked pretty happy too.

From that moment on, Swoop and Mogli
became **inseparable**.

The pair would cuddle, and sometimes they
would fall asleep together.

Swoop followed Mogli everywhere he went ...

and when Swoop finally grew her flight feathers,
she and Mogli went on adventures together.

One day, when they were wandering along the beach,
they saw a beautiful

kingfisher.

And Swoop began to wonder . . .

was she a **human**, like dad Matt?

Was she a **cat**, like brother Mogli?

Or was she a **bird**, like the tūī in the trees,
or that kingfisher they had seen?

The next day, Swoop visited the kingfisher. It had **feathers**, just like her. It had a **beak**, just like her. And it could **fly** . . . just like her.

"Am I like you?" Swoop asked.

"Well, you are a **bird** like me," said the kingfisher, "but you have different feathers – and you're bigger than me. But there are some magpies further down the road that look a lot like you. Why don't you ask them?"

So off Swoop flew,
in search of the birds that looked like her.

Further down the road she came across the neighbourhood kids.
They played with her for a while, but she knew she was different from them.

Swoop flew high in the sky, soaring over fields and past the lighthouse. Nowhere could she see the family of magpies she had been told about.

Then, just as she was about to turn back, she spotted them.
They were just like her, with the same glossy black and white feathers.

Surely they must be her family, she thought, but she was too shy to go nearer.

That night, as Swoop cuddled into Mogli on Matt's bed, she couldn't stop thinking about the family of magpies she had seen that day.

When she woke up the next morning, she knew she had to go and introduce herself.

Swoop flew down the road, across the fields, and past the lighthouse until she reached the magpie family. Bravely, she landed on a branch in their midst.

The magpies were very welcoming, and Swoop felt at home with them. **Could they be my real family?** she wondered.

Swoop thought about Matt and Mogli and how
they had cared for her in their little house by the sea.

She thought about how they had gone on adventures together.

Just like family.

But now . . .

Yes, she knew it now. The magpies were her family too.

Swoop was sad to think she was leaving Matt and brother Mogli, but she knew it was time to start her journey with her new family.

At that moment, the family of magpies took off into the skies. Swoop hesitated, then squawked, **"Wait for me! I'm coming too!"**

And as Swoop flew over the house she'd grown up in, she felt sad, but excited.

In her heart, Swoop knew she had made the right choice.

But sometimes – just sometimes – she still pays a visit to her first home by the sea.

A note from Matt Owens

Swoop and I crossed paths when we needed each other most. She was injured and needed help, and I needed something to keep my mind occupied with positive things after receiving some tragic news from my father regarding his health. I already had a cat called Mogli and I had no idea how he would react to a baby magpie joining the family. Swoop made it through the first night and I decided to introduce the two. Mogli was instantly curious and, whilst I was cautious initially, I soon found that I could trust him. The pair from then on were inseparable, best mates, hanging out together, often snuggled up fast asleep.

I loved watching Swoop learn to walk. Then, watching her feathers mature and watching her slowly start to fly was something I'll never forget. Swoop was always free to come and go as she pleased and with a simple whistle I could summon her from wherever she was — sometimes far, far away — and suddenly she would land on my shoulder. I would play fetch with her, she would sing along with me while I played the guitar, she even accompanied me on long walks around the bays.

Swoop made many friends in the neighbourhood of the human variety. One of those friends was Emma Gustafson, an artist I hadn't yet met at that time. It wasn't until Swoop left the nest that I learned of their friendship and met Emma for myself. That's how *The Story of Swoop* was born.